THE
BIG
RIVERS

THE BIG RIVERS

The Missouri, the Mississippi, and the Ohio

Written and illustrated by Bruce Hiscock

Atheneum Books for Young Readers

BOOKS BY BRUCE HISCOCK

Tundra   The Big Storm

The Big Rock   When Will It Snow?

The Big Tree   The Big Rivers

Atheneum Books for Young Readers
An imprint of Simon & Schuster Children's Publishing Division
1230 Avenue of the Americas
New York, New York 10020

Book design by Virginia Pope
The text of this book is set in Candida.
The illustrations are rendered in watercolor.

First Edition
Printed in the United States of America
10 9 8 7 6 5 4 3 2 1

Library of Congress Cataloging-in-Publication Data
Hiscock, Bruce.
The big rivers: the Missouri, the Mississippi, and the Ohio /
written and illustrated by Bruce Hiscock.—1st ed.
p. cm.
Summary: Describes the conditions that led up to the
severe flooding in the Mississippi River valley in 1993.
ISBN 0-689-80871-2
1. Floods—Mississippi River Valley—Juvenile literature.
[1. Floods—Mississippi River Valley.] I. Title.
GB1399.4.M7H57   1997
551.48.'9'0977—dc20
96-2435

Heavy Rain
Minnesota,
Iowa, Wisconsin
Floods Begin

More Rain
Barge Traffic
Slows, then
stops

Frequent rains soak the Midwestern soil

'RAI

MAY

JUNE

20 feet

Flood Wall 22 feet

Mississippi River
water level at St. Louis.

10 feet

flood stage

*To all those who worked on
the Great Flood of '93*

Drenching Rain
in Iowa floods
Des Moines

...ACHINE" pours down

JULY

Rainfall eases, still above normal

AUGUST

↑First Flood Crest

Second Crest
19.6 feet above
flood stage

Old Record Level
1973 Flood

THE GREAT FLOOD OF 1993

pring is an uncertain time for people who live near the big rivers: the Missouri, the Mississippi, and the Ohio. These rivers cross the center of the United States, and each spring when the snow begins to melt and the rains return, the rivers start to rise. Small streams may swell quickly from the runoff, but the big rivers react in slow motion. The swirling water comes up quietly, steadily, and with enormous power. Then families watch from the riverbanks, hoping the water will not rise too fast and bring another disastrous flood.

When spring arrived in 1993, no serious flooding was expected on the big rivers. It had been an average winter, and the snow that remained was not especially deep.

Out West, in cattle country, a brilliant March sun was melting the snow on the mountains of Montana. Ribbons of icy water ran down the slopes to form brooks and roaring streams that flowed into the beginning of the Missouri River. The big river rose gently as the water began its long journey to the sea.

Farther east, in Minnesota, it was raining. A steady patter of cold drops fell on the fields and forests, and splashed on the highways. The ground was still soggy from thawing snow, so the rain could not soak in. Instead, it ran along the surface, carrying with it bits of soil, salt, and fertilizers. The rainwater filled the ditches and then found its way through the swamps and creeks to the upper part of the Mississippi River.

In the hills of West Virginia, the snow was already gone.
There, a school class was visiting an electric power plant on the
Ohio River. Before getting on the bus, everyone used the
bathrooms and everyone flushed, like thousands of other
people in the valley. That water was now flowing past them as
a tiny part of the third big river, the Ohio.

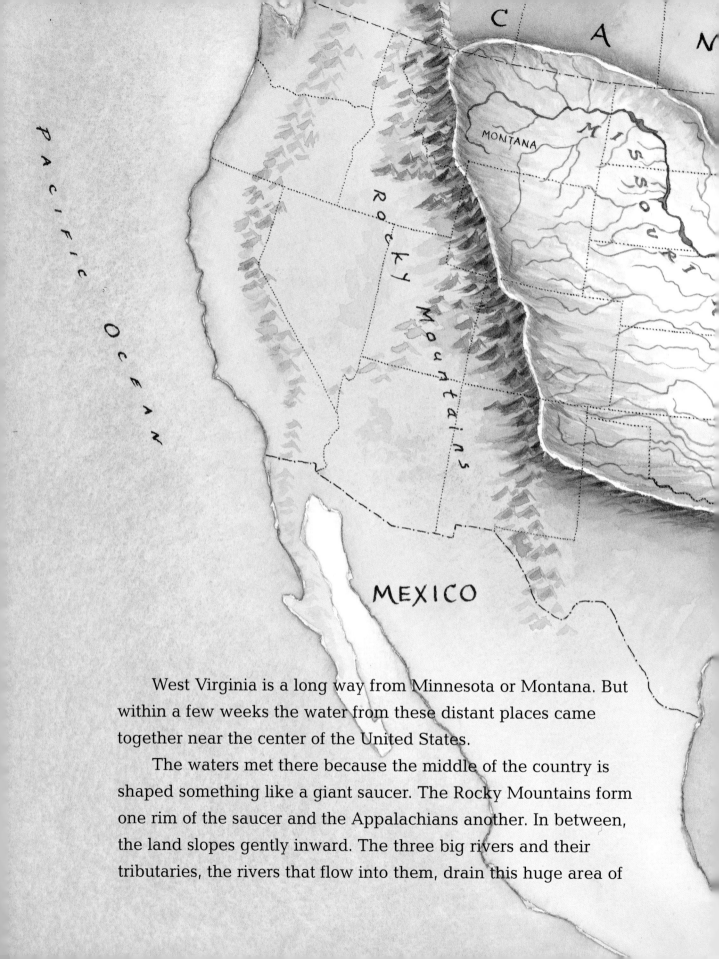

West Virginia is a long way from Minnesota or Montana. But within a few weeks the water from these distant places came together near the center of the United States.

The waters met there because the middle of the country is shaped something like a giant saucer. The Rocky Mountains form one rim of the saucer and the Appalachians another. In between, the land slopes gently inward. The three big rivers and their tributaries, the rivers that flow into them, drain this huge area of

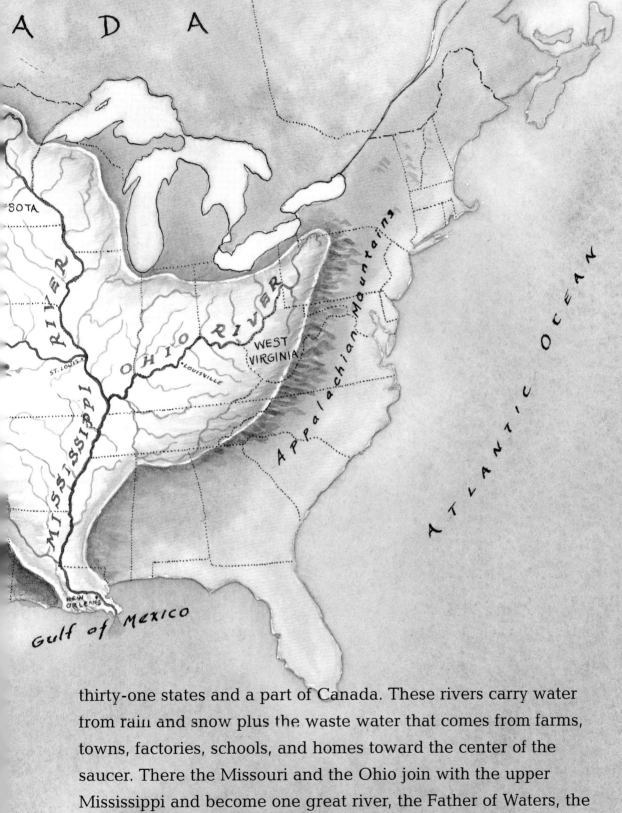

thirty-one states and a part of Canada. These rivers carry water from rain and snow plus the waste water that comes from farms, towns, factories, schools, and homes toward the center of the saucer. There the Missouri and the Ohio join with the upper Mississippi and become one great river, the Father of Waters, the mighty Mississippi. The Mississippi then flows south to the Gulf of Mexico, the lowest spot on the saucer's rim.

This is the third largest drainage basin in the world. Where so much water comes together, floods are fairly common. Nearly every year some stretch of river will overflow its banks. Most of these floods are minor, but a few times each century enormous floods occur.

As spring continued in 1993, the ice broke up in the North, and there was some flooding. But before long, barges were again carrying coal down the Ohio and wheat on the Mississippi and Missouri. Farmers began their spring planting. Kids talked about summer vacation and swimming. Stories of the last big flood, in 1973, were like ancient history to them, and not even their parents suspected what was coming.

Normal

Flood

A long time ago, when the country was mostly wilderness, floods were not a problem. If a river rose above its banks, the water simply spilled out onto the floodplain, the flat land that lies next to the river channel. For a while the floodplains became shallow lakes.

When the river went down, the shallow lakes drained back into the riverbed. The flooded land was a muddy mess after the water receded, but the soil was actually improved by the silt the river left behind. This is why the floodplain, or bottomland as it is sometimes called, makes such good farmland. Indians grew crops of corn, squash, and beans there long before European explorers even found the rivers.

As settlers moved west, however, things began to change. There were few roads in that part of the land, and so the rivers, where big catfish and sturgeon swam, served as the best routes to the frontier. As the river traffic increased, towns like Louisville, New Orleans, and St. Louis were built on the banks.

By the mid-1800s, the country was growing fast, and fancy steamboats hauled cotton, lumber, and other goods up and down the broad rivers. Where Indians had grown a few crops in the black dirt of the bottomlands, farmers now planted large fields.

The spring floods became a nuisance to boats, a danger to river towns, and the enemy to farmers. And so, people began to think of ways to control the big rivers.

Levees, artificial high banks of earth, were built along the rivers to protect the farms and towns on the floodplain. Later, dams were constructed across the Missouri, and also on many tributaries. These dams were designed to hold back floodwaters, to generate electricity from the flow of the river, and to store water for irrigation, that is, water used to grow crops on the dry prairies.

Other dams and locks were built on the upper Mississippi and the Ohio to make sure the navigation channel would always be nine feet deep. That is just deep enough for the rafts of barges, called tows, that now carry most river freight, and the powerful boats that push them.

The control of the rivers began with a few levees in the 1800s. By 1993 there were hundreds of dams and thousands of miles of levees guarding against floods.

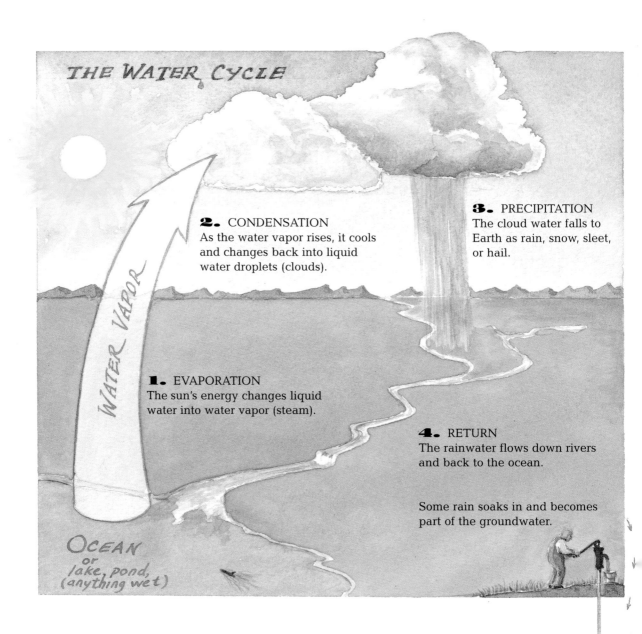

THE WATER CYCLE

2. CONDENSATION
As the water vapor rises, it cools and changes back into liquid water droplets (clouds).

3. PRECIPITATION
The cloud water falls to Earth as rain, snow, sleet, or hail.

WATER VAPOR

1. EVAPORATION
The sun's energy changes liquid water into water vapor (steam).

4. RETURN
The rainwater flows down rivers and back to the ocean.

Some rain soaks in and becomes part of the groundwater.

OCEAN
or lake, pond, (anything wet)

As spring turned into summer that year, it began to rain hard in the Midwest. Rain is the lifeblood of rivers and a part of the water cycle. All rivers are created from water that evaporates, mostly from the ocean, and then falls back on the land as rain and snow. The water then flows down the rivers to the ocean, completing the cycle. When the weather is normal, the rivers can easily handle the flow, and the water cycle goes on without much notice.

THE RAIN MACHINE

COLD AIR

MISSOURI RIVER →

MISSISSIPPI RIVER →

OHIO RIVER

WARM MOIST AIR

But in the summer of 1993, the normal weather pattern in the Midwest changed. Humid air, full of moisture from the Gulf of Mexico, streamed north creating massive thunderstorms as it clashed with cool air from Canada. This "rain machine" stalled over Iowa, Missouri, and neighboring states, drenching some places with two to five inches of rain each day. At the same time along the Ohio River, where it is usually quite rainy, the weather was dry.

In late June, flooding started in Minnesota and Iowa sending the first crest of high water down the Mississippi. A warning call went out. Levees were checked. Supplies of sandbags and sand were prepared. Families who lived in low areas got ready to move.

Then, as if to tease everyone, the rain slacked off for a while, only to come back harder than ever. The lower Missouri River pushed over its banks, flooding thousands of acres of farmland with two or three feet of water.

People began to build dams of sandbags to save buildings close to the river. Volunteers, including kids and grandparents, turned out to help. National Guard troops and prison crews were brought in as the rain continued.

NO PARKING HERE

Smaller rivers rose quickly now. The surging Raccoon River in Des Moines, Iowa, flooded the water purification plant despite the seventeen-foot-high levee protecting it. In Des Moines, there was water everywhere, but none of it was fit to drink.

Along the Mississippi, a record flood was building, and the rain would not stop. Families moved their couches and refrigerators upstairs, and then left their homes, taking whatever they could. In many river towns the neighborhoods without levees were covered with water by mid-July.

Still the rain kept coming. Riverbanks caved in, and whole trees were swept along in the swift current as the water rose. Soon the river was nearing the top of the long levees that guard the farms on the floodplains. Radio stations asked for more people to help sandbag, and more volunteers came.

They worked in the heat and rain, filling woven plastic bags with three shovel-scoops of sand, and then hoisting them on a truck or boat or helicopter to take to the levee. Restaurants donated pizza, sandwiches, and tacos for the workers. Cases of canned water arrived from beer and soft drink companies. It was hard labor, but the volunteers kept at it, and a wall of sandbags grew along miles and miles of levees.

The work went on until the sandbags were piled high. But the earthen farm levees were never meant to hold back the river this long, and they were dangerously weak. Each night, crews walked quietly along the levees, checking for seepage and patching the leaks with straw and sandbags. The power of Old Man River in flood is overwhelming. One by one the farm levees failed, and the river spilled in, covering green fields of corn and soy beans with brown, muddy water.

Near the cities, the levees were higher and stronger. At St. Louis, where the Mississippi and Missouri meet, the water rose to almost twenty feet above flood stage, but the concrete floodwall, built for twenty-two feet, held, and most of the town stayed dry.

The flooding was some of the worst ever seen on the Missouri and Mississippi rivers. Over one hundred thousand homes, stores, and factories were flooded, along with vast areas of farmland. People and animals were drowned. Miles of roads and railroad tracks were washed away. Bridges were closed. Plants that treat waste water became overloaded from the rain, forcing towns to let raw sewage flow into the rivers. Since many towns take their drinking water from the rivers, extra precautions were needed to make the water safe to use.

The great flood of '93 lasted longer than most floods—over a month in some places. But eventually the storms ended, and then the enormous job of cleaning up the smelly, soggy mess began. It wasn't much fun, but floods have always been a part of life along the river.

Fortunately the dry weather continued in the eastern United States. This cut back the flow of the Ohio River, which usually carries twice as much water as the Missouri and upper Mississippi combined. And so there was room for extra water in the broad channel of the lower Mississippi River, downstream from the Ohio. When the floodwater coming down from St. Louis reached that point, it went back to the riverbed. From there on, the Mississippi stayed within its banks and levees, and the southern states were not flooded at all.

As the muddy water flowed south toward the sea, it followed the winding course of the lower Mississippi. There the big river meanders in great looping bends over a floodplain many miles wide. In years past, the river would sometimes cut a new channel across one of the bends leaving the old bend behind as an oxbow lake. Towns that were shipping ports could be left miles from the river by these sudden changes in the channel.

Now all the big river channels are fixed and controlled. The United States Army Corps of Engineers is in charge of keeping the rivers in place. The network of dams and levees works well against smaller floods. A flood the size of the 1993 disaster is only expected once every few hundred years.

OXBOW LAKE

Farther south the river flows past fields of cotton and corn. Then in Louisiana, the riverbank farms are replaced by chemical plants and petroleum refineries. Here the river channel has been dredged deeper to allow ocean-going tankers to come upstream. After passing New Orleans, the Mississippi finally reaches the sea.

When the big river enters the ocean it drops millions of tons of sand and soil—the fine silt it always carries. Over the ages this river sediment has formed an enormous delta of marsh, beach, and dry land at the mouth of the river. In fact, much of Louisiana is actually river delta, land created from soil brought by the river from the plains and prairies to the north.

The water that returns to the ocean down the big rivers has gone through the water cycle countless times, for most water is billions of years old. It has fallen as rain on mountains that no longer exist and traveled down rivers that humans never saw. Perhaps the water in your faucet once flowed in the Congo or the Amazon, or was gulped by a dinosaur. This constant recycling of water is the source of all rivers. All life on this watery planet, including us, depends on this endless cycle.

AUTHOR'S NOTE

I made three trips to the rivers while working on this book. Once, I waded across the Mississippi where it is just a brook coming out of Lake Itasca in Minnesota. The stones on the bottom did not feel smooth like natural river gravel.

A sign explained that, originally, the Mississippi began as a swampy outflow from the lake. That was considered undignified for the source of an important river, so a channel was dredged through the cattails and lined with tons of crushed stone.

This is a tiny example of how we have altered (and lost) about half of the wetlands in the United States. These marshy areas store and filter water before it goes into the ground or down the rivers, and they are home to many plants and animals. The changes at Lake Itasca are minor, but the draining of thousands of acres of wetlands for farms, buildings, and parking lots has had major effects. Now there is more runoff, flooding occurs faster, our water is less pure, and we have lost valuable wildlife habitat.

I traveled to the rivers again at the height of the flood. For several days I filled sandbags, took photos, and drew sketches.

Being there is quite different from watching the flood on TV. People seem much calmer, and there is real satisfaction in working together. The power of the river is so apparent that when a levee fails it is accepted with a kind of quiet reverence.

On my third trip I drove down the Ohio and Mississippi to the Gulf of Mexico. I talked with farmers, librarians, kids, people fishing, boat crews, and the engineers at the Waterways Experiment Station in Vicksburg, Mississippi.

As we spoke about the problems of pollution and river management, I began to see how complex our environmental issues have become. One thing was clear, though. We have gained control (but not mastery) over much of what happens in our water and air. We are no longer a nation of pioneers living at the mercy of nature. Now it is the other way around.